MW00965366

MYRA C. HARRIS

Recipes and Fantasies

How To
Get
A Man

From The Kitchen,
To The Bedroom,
To The Ring

PUBLISHED BY
LeTay Publishing
ATLANTA

2014

Published by
LeTay Publishing
P.O. Box 170233
Atlanta, Georgia 30317
404-667-2810
booksales@letaypublishing.com
www.letaypublishing.com

How To Get A Man...

FROM THE KITCHEN, TO THE BEDROOM, TO THE RING

Recipes and Fantasies

The body text for this book is Helvetica Neue Regular and Bickley Script LET with titles in Zapfino and Copperplate.

PRINTED IN THE UNITED STATES

Library of Congress Cataloging-in-Publication Data
Harris, Myra Celesta
How To Get A Man: From the Kitchen, To the Bedroom, To the Ring
Written by Myra Celesta Harris

ISBN-13 978-0-9830731-6-1

1. Adult Fiction   2. Romance   3. Cookbook
Adult

$19.95

This book is dedicated to my late father, Mr. Floyd R. Harris and my beautiful mother, Mrs. Fay E. Harris, who both loved cooking at home and in the church. I never realized the joy and happiness that food could bring to a person's soul until I started cooking myself.

Mom and Dad, thanks so much for showing me happiness in the most simplistic ways. Daddy, thanks for your creativity and Momma, thanks for being the stylish diva that you are. I couldn't have written this book without you both. And to my amazing son, Darius, thanks for being such a blessing! I love you all!

JERRA, I HOPE THAT YOU APPRECIATE MY CREATIVITY! PLEASE ENJOY!

Myra C.

This book focuses on all the things that exude sexiness—yes, in the kitchen. I have created some exciting fantasies, provided a complete menu, which includes step-by-step recipes, along with music and drink suggestions, so that you can create the perfect evening for you and your significant other. And, might I add, that I am making these fantasies come true, while wearing my sexy apron, makeup, perfume and various sexy, strappy sandals—yes, that's right. I've also included some food for thought through the **Tempt Your Senses** callouts, which you will see in several chapters. This information lets you know about foods that have an aphrodisiac composition and how they can enhance your menu. **Tempt Your Senses** tells you what the food is and what makes it so sensual.

This book is a guide that walks you through the positive ways to master the art of courtship with food, caring and sex appeal. What is courtship, you ask? As defined by **Merriam-Webster.com**, *it is the act of paying attention to somebody with a view to developing a more intimate relationship.* This can also be a very rich, nurturing, beautiful and growing experience.

Are you ready for a lasting relationship? Can you handle it? Because if you're ready, I've got something to share with you that will make you a better friend, a better lover and even a better cook.

I welcome you to **How to Get a Man From the Kitchen, To the Bedroom, To the Ring. Recipes & Fantasies**! Please Enjoy! And I hope *your* Fantasies come true!

Fantasy #1
HIS BIG PROMOTION

My special gentleman and I have been dating for a year and he has just been promoted to Executive Vice President at his pharmaceutical company. I've invited him over for dinner, but he doesn't know it's a celebration for his promotion. Now what can I pull out of my big bag of tricks for a surprise dinner?

I know what—his favorites and some of my specialties— Say My Name Baby Back Ribs, Ready or Not Barbecue Sauce, I'm Bossy Red Skinned Mashed Potatoes, some delicious 12 Play Garlic Roasted Asparagus and for dessert—an irresistible Scandalous Banana Split.

So off to the store I go to grab the ingredients and then I'll dash home to prep for dinner. With all this preparation, I can't forget that the main ingredient for tonight is me.

I need to make sure that I'm looking my Divalicious best. I've given it some thought and I just remembered a spicy pair of stilettos that he hasn't seen. And I know that he loves to see me in red lipstick. Now that I have the menu and my glam in order, let's start my gentleman's meal. I'd better hurry because it will take a few hours for the ribs. It's now 5 o'clock and he will be here in 2 hours. . .

Say My Name Baby Back Ribs

Makes 2 large servings or 4 small servings

Prep Time: 30 minutes
Cooking Time: 2½ hours

Ingredients:
1 rack pork baby back ribs [3 pounds]

Rib Dry Rub

Prep time: 5 minutes

Ingredients:
2 tablespoons seasoned salt
1 tablespoon mustard powder
1 tablespoon onion powder
1 tablespoon paprika
2 tablespoons kosher salt
1 teaspoon chili powder

1 teaspoon black pepper

1 teaspoon brown sugar

½ teaspoon cayenne pepper

Instructions:

1. Rinse and remove any excess fat from the ribs (as needed).
2. Combine the dry rub ingredients into a small bowl, then stir to mix.
3. Sprinkle the meat on both sides with the rub, patting the spices in with your fingers.
4. Preheat oven to 375 degrees F.
5. Tear off 4 pieces of aluminum foil, long enough to enclose each portion of ribs. Spray each piece of foil with vegetable oil cooking spray. Wrap tightly and place on a cookie sheet (lined with parchment paper).
6. Bake for 2 hours, remove from the aluminum foil, baste with barbecue sauce and place back in the oven for 30 minutes.

Ready or Not Barbecue Sauce

Prep Time: 10 minutes

Cooking Time: 20-25 minutes

Ingredients:

1 cup Jack Daniels Barbecue Sauce

¼ cup brown sugar

¼ teaspoon cayenne pepper

½ cup Jack Daniels whiskey

Instructions:

1. In a large saucepan, combine the barbecue sauce, brown sugar, cayenne pepper and whiskey.
2. Mix well and bring to a low simmer for 20-25 minutes until the sauce is combined.

Now that the Ribs are cooking nicely in the oven, I'll work on the wonderful, delicious sides.

I'm Bossy Red Skinned Mashed Potatoes with Cheese
Makes 4 servings
Prep Time: 20 minutes
Cooking Time: 20-25 minutes

Ingredients:
2 pounds red potatoes
3 tablespoons butter
½ cup milk or heavy cream
¼ cup shredded cheddar cheese
Salt and pepper to taste

Instructions:

1. Rinse potatoes, remove any bad spots and cut into quarters.
2. Bring a pot of salted water to a boil. Add potatoes and cook for 20-25 minutes. Remove from the stove and drain using a colander.

3. Mash the potatoes using potato masher or electric mixer until smooth, adding butter and milk until combined. Toss in the cheese, then add salt and pepper to taste.

12 Play Garlic Roasted Asparagus

Makes 4 servings

Prep Time: 5 minutes

Cooking Time: 12 to 15 minutes (Can vary depending on the size of the asparagus)

Ingredients:

1 pound green asparagus

2 tablespoons extra virgin olive oil

2 teaspoons minced garlic

½ teaspoon salt

½ teaspoon pepper

Instructions:

1. Preheat oven to 425 degrees F.
2. Rinse and clean the asparagus heads (ensuring that any possible debris has been removed).
3. Hold both ends of the asparagus and bend; it will snap in half. The top portion is edible; discard the bottom portion.
4. Mix olive oil and garlic in a bowl, then massage all over the asparagus.
5. Sprinkle with salt and pepper.
6. Place into a baking dish and roast for 12 to 15 minutes, turning over a few times until the asparagus is tender.

Tempt Your Senses

Asparagus The phallic shape of some foods is a consideration in the selection of aphrodisiac foods. However, asparagus has more to offer than its suggestive form. It contains vitamin E, which is believed to stimulate sex hormones which contribute to a healthy sex life and increased sexual powers. *Courtesy of www.fuelthemind.com*

It's 6:25 and now while the ribs and asparagus are cooking, it's time to get my glam on. Into the shower I go, definitely using one of my scented shower gels to add a nice fragrance in the air. Shower finished and now on to drying off, taking extra care in applying a scented lotion, French perfume and flawless makeup with perfect lips. It's amazing what red lipstick does to a man!

Now let me grab my attire for the evening—my Sexy Apron, of course, and sexy, beaded stilettos . . . oh my goodness, what am I getting myself into tonight? I hope my gentleman is ready for some good food and me.

It's 7:05 and my gentleman has arrived with flowers in hand. I graciously thank him and place the flowers in a vase. They fit so beautifully on the dining room table. He can't believe the aroma coming from the kitchen. "Is that your wonderful Say My Name Baby Back Ribs?" He asked with excitement in his voice. "Yes, dear, . . .it's all of your favorites." I answer with a satisfied and sexy voice. I'm glad he enjoys my cooking. "I prepared this special meal to show you just how proud I am of you. I have some time before everything is ready, so I'll prepare dessert—my irresistible Scandalous Banana Split." He offers. "May I give you a hand?" "No, dear, just sit down and relax." I've noticed that he can't keep his eyes off me in the kitchen.

Scandalous Banana Split

Makes 2 servings

Prep Time: 10 minutes

Cooking Time: 30 minutes refrigeration

Ingredients:

2 bananas, cut lengthwise (then cut in half)

2 scoops of butter pecan (his favorite)

2 tablespoons chocolate syrup (or hot fudge)

½ cup fresh strawberries, cut into hearty slices

2 tablespoons chopped nuts

A dollop (spoon full) of whipped cream

Instructions:

1. Place the bananas along the side of an oval bowl or dish.
2. Place the scoops of ice cream in the center of the bowl.
3. Add the toppings (chocolate, strawberries and nuts) to enhance the flavor and color of the dessert.
4. This wouldn't be complete without topping it with a dollop of whipped cream and a maraschino cherry or two.
5. Place in the refrigerator (to stay chilled) until after dinner.

Tempt Your Senses

Bananas Bananas have a wonderful, suggestive phallic shape, and are considered one of the most popular aphrodisiac foods used to stimulate sexual desire and increase sexual powers. Bananas also contain potassium and B vitamins which are essential for sex hormone production. *Courtesy of www.fuelthemind.com*

Dinner is ready! I've made our plates and placed them on the dining room table alongside my beautiful flowers. The food is blessed and we begin to dine and converse while enjoying this home-cooked meal.

An hour has passed and we are still enjoying the ambiance, conversation and food. I remind him, "My dear gentleman, let's not forget dessert." I grab one of my Scandalous Banana Splits from the fridge. There's only one spoon needed for this treat. I begin to feed him this divine dessert, one spoonful at a time. Halfway through dessert, he thanks me for the most beautiful, thoughtful and romantic evening. He then tells me that he hasn't been able to focus since he arrived and saw me wearing my sexy apron, stilettos and his favorite lipstick. He whispers to me, "Come with me. Now I want to do something for you."

Drink Suggestion(s)

Cater to You Peach Lemonade

Makes 2 drinks

Prep Time: 10 minutes

Ingredients:

6 ounces Peach flavored vodka

6 ounces Lemonade

Sliced Orange, Lemon or Peach for Garnish

Instructions:

1. Shake the vodka and lemonade well with ice; then strain into a chilled glass filled with ice.
2. Garnish with a piece of fresh fruit.

Music Suggestion(s)

There You Go—Johnny Gill

Let's Chill—Guy

There's a Meeting In My Bedroom—Silk

Nothing Has Ever Felt Like This—Rachelle Ferrell and Will Downing

Forever, For Always, For Love—Lalah Hathaway

Forever My Lady—Jodeci

You & I—Avant & Keke Wyatt

Fantasy #2
MOVIE NIGHT

It's Tuesday afternoon and I just left my client's office headed for home. I had a great day and in a few hours, I will prepare dinner for me and my gentleman's weekly movie night. We typically watch action, mysteries, horror or love stories. Our schedules are very busy these days, but we always try to keep our movie night.

So, I've made it home and now I need to shower and gather all the ingredients for tonight's Movie Night Dinner. What will it be? It's a chilly evening, so let's go with something hearty. I know the exact meal . . . my Come Share My Love Spaghetti and Meat Sauce, some All For You Garlic Bread and for dessert, my Body Party Strawberry Milkshakes.

I've gathered all the ingredients from my pantry and

fridge, bagged them and now into the shower I go. I'm so excited about seeing my gentleman tonight, as it's been a week and I really do miss him. I've jumped out the shower and now let's give myself a simple facial before applying my makeup. My makeup looks flawless, including a natural lip gloss and let's not forget that I've applied a little bit of glitter (here and there) to make everything pop!

So, what do I wear, as it's chilly outside on this February evening? I'll put on my black wrap around dress that's low cut and stops a few inches shy of my knee, my knee high boots, some French perfume and of course, my sexy apron.

The bagged groceries are packed into the car and I'm headed to my gentleman's house. Because I have keys, its straight into the kitchen I go, but before getting started, let me slip into my sexy apron.

This delicious meal will take about an hour to prepare. So I get a head start on my Come Share My Love Spaghetti Sauce because my gentleman should be home in about the same time.

Come Share My Love Spaghetti Sauce

Makes 4 to 6 servings

Prep Time: 20-25 minutes

Cooking Time: 1 hour

Ingredients:

1 pound ground beef

1 pound hot Italian sausage

1 large onion, chopped

2 bell peppers, chopped

1 teaspoon minced garlic

2 (29 oz.) cans tomato sauce

1 (14.5 oz.) can diced tomatoes

1 cup sliced mushrooms

2 tablespoons sugar

1 tablespoon Italian seasoning

½ cup chicken broth

½ cup red wine

1 teaspoon pepper

1 teaspoon salt

Instructions:

1. Add olive oil in a large skillet over medium heat; add onion and bell peppers and cook, stirring constantly, until tender, about 5-6 minutes. Add garlic; cook, stirring constantly, for 1 minute. Add the mixture to large saucepan that will contain spaghetti sauce.

2. In the same warm skillet, add ground beef and sausage,

cook, stirring until meat crumbles and no more pink appears; drain. Add to large saucepan for spaghetti sauce. Stir in the tomato sauce and the next 8 ingredients.

4. Simmer on low heat for 60 minutes, stirring occasionally. Cool.

Note: The sauce will keep for several days covered and refrigerated. Serve with spaghetti or your favorite pasta.

Jungle Love Spaghetti

Makes 2 to 4 servings

Prep Time: 5 minutes

Cooking Time: 6-8 minutes

Ingredients:

1 pound spaghetti

1 teaspoon salt

1 teaspoon extra virgin olive oil

Instructions:

1. Drizzle the olive oil into a large pot of boiling water. Add salt.
2. Add spaghetti to the boiling water. Allow to cook for 6-8 minutes, stirring occasionally until al dente.
3. Drain into a colander.

I hear my gentleman's key in the door. He walks in and compliments me on looking sexy and for the wonderful aroma coming from the kitchen. He exits to change out of his suit and put on something comfortable.

Now that the spaghetti is done and while the sauce is still simmering, I'll prepare the All For You Garlic Bread and our dessert, the Body Party Strawberry Milkshake.

Tempt Your Senses

Raspberries and strawberries These are perfect aphrodisiac foods to hand feed your lover. They are red, which is the color associated with love and passion, and are high in vitamin C. *Courtesy of www.fuelthemind.com*

All For You Garlic Bread

Makes 6 servings

Prep Time:	10 minutes
Cooking Time:	12 minutes

Ingredients:

1 (½ pound) loaf Italian Bread, cut into 1 inch slices

5 tablespoons butter, softened

2 teaspoons extra virgin olive oil

3 teaspoons minced garlic

1 teaspoon dried parsley

¼ cup pepper jack cheese (optional)

Instructions:

1. Preheat oven to 350 degrees F.
2. In a small bowl, mix butter, olive oil and garlic.
3. Place bread on a baking sheet with parchment paper.
4. Spread mixture evenly on each slice of bread, and then sprinkle with parsley.
5. Bake for approximately 8 minutes. Remove from the oven. Spread the remainder of the butter mixture and sprinkle with pepper jack cheese, if desired.
6. Place back in the oven and broil for 2 minutes, or until cheese is melted.

Body Party Strawberry Milkshake

Makes 2 servings

Prep time: 10 minutes

Ingredients:

2 cups strawberry ice cream

2 cups vanilla ice cream

½ cup fresh or frozen strawberries, thawed

½ cup milk

2 teaspoons vanilla extract

Instructions:

1. Combine all ingredients in container of an electric blender; process until smooth.
2. Serve in tall glasses with a straw.
3. Place in refrigerator to keep cold until ready to serve.

My gentleman comes into the kitchen and opens a bottle of my favorite Italian Moscato and pours me a glass. "Here's to you babe for always catering to me." He salutes me. I reply, "It's my pleasure." "So what are we watching tonight?" He asks. I reply, "How about an action packed movie or perhaps a comedy?"

"Whatever you want princess. I picked the last movie, so tonight is your night." He's so gracious that it makes me blush. I decide. "Comedy it is." I prepare our plates and we decide to dine in the bar area of my gentleman's home theater. He blesses the food and we begin to converse a few minutes before starting the movie. He replies, "Wow, this is perfect food for this cold evening and can't wait to taste it. It looks and smells amazing."

We have a lot to catch up on, as it's been a week since we've seen each other, so we are engaged in deep conversation. The movie is playing in the background and we are enjoying each other's company, the food and the wine.

We decide to stop the movie, as we are being more entertained by each other than the movie. He selects some nice music and I prepare dessert—the Body Party Strawberry Milkshakes.

He responds, "These milkshakes are delicious and I can really taste the fresh strawberries." We enjoy dessert and chat for another 30 minutes or so, until he asks me to dance. We dance a few songs and he says he has *a gift for me. "Wait here Princess, I'll be right back."*

To my surprise and delight he returns with a warm bottle of honey . . . and a big smile.

Tempt Your Senses

Wine Wine relaxes our inhibitions and stimulates our senses. The actual drinking of wine can be an erotic experience. Moderate amounts of wine are believed to arouse or leave a momentary flush in your face, but excessive alcohol will make you drowsy. *Courtesy of www.fuelthemind.com*

Drink Suggestion(s)

A nice bottle or 2 of Red Wine

Music Suggestion(s)

Somewhere in My Lifetime—Phyllis Hyman

Do You Love What you Feel—Chaka Khan

You Can't Hide Love—Earth, Wind & Fire

Insatiable—Prince

Shining Star—The Manhattans

Whatever it Takes—Anita Baker

Tonight Is The Night—Betty Wright

Fantasy #3
OUR VACATION

The day has finally arrived for our Caribbean vacation. My gentleman and I are headed to the airport for our much needed, 7-day luxurious vacation in Turks & Caicos. We've made it through security and are now patiently awaiting to board our flight. We've both been working so hard and are looking forward to spending this quality time together.

Our flight is finally starting to board and 1st class—here we come. After comfortably being seated, we gesture to our flight attendant that we are ready to start our vacation and each want a glass of mimosa. The attendant adheres to our request and two mimosas appear on our tray tables. We lift our glasses and my gentleman makes a toast, "Cheers to 7 days of us time." We indulge in another mimosa before our flight departs. We are both very relaxed and enjoying small talk, awaiting our descent into Turks & Caicos. It's 12:45pm in the afternoon and we have safely landed. What a lover's paradise? The weather is warm; the sun is bright and the islanders are happily greeting us. Welcome! Welcome! Welcome!

Our driver meets us at baggage claim to grab our bags and it's off to our luxurious villa we go. En route to our villa, we notice the beautiful beaches, shops and the amazing smell of grilled fish. We both love seafood and during our flight, we talked about indulging in a lot of it during our vacation. We decide to have the driver stop so that we can grab some grilled fish for lunch. We are so hungry that we can't wait to get to the villa before devouring the fish. And, oh how good it is? The fish melts right in your mouth and is so moist and flavorful—the onions, hot peppers and the special sauce—it's amazing! We have both decided that we will definitely pay this restaurant another visit while we are here.

The driver tells us that we are only 5 minutes away from the villa. We continue to enjoy the picturesque island, as we snap pictures along the way. The driver turns off the main road and slowly approaches a gated property. We can't believe what we're seeing. A palatial villa—7,000 square feet of luxury to be exact—amidst the turquoise waters and pristine white sand beaches, a large gazebo, fresh water swimming pool and a marble hot tub. My, my, my and we haven't even made it inside.

The villa's staff greets us at the door and gives us a tour, while the driver brings in our bags. A gourmet, custom kitchen, marble floors, vaulted ceilings, a custom barbecue grill on the deck, and let's not forget our bedroom with a private terrace overlooking the pool and ocean—all for my gentleman and I to enjoy. We decide to take a quick shower, change our clothes and have drinks out on our bedroom terrace.

Three hours have passed and we are still enjoying each other's company, as well as, the ocean view and the beautiful weather. Now we are getting a little hungry because it's been 5 hours since we enjoyed the wonderful fish. What will it be for dinner? I've got an idea. I can prepare my Whip Appeal Grilled Spiny Lobster Tails with Bad Mamma Jamma Rum Butter Sauce, a delicious How Does It Feel Tropical Salad and Somebody Loves You Baby Grilled Rum Cake. My gentleman responds, "That is a sexy meal." What he doesn't know is that when I coordinated our travel, I requested that the needed ingredients be stocked in the fridge and the bar ready with our favorite beverages.

First things first, let me grab my sexy apron and yes, I packed it. "Princess, do you need any help?" "No dear not right now. I want you to just relax and enjoy your drinks while I prepare dinner, but I think dessert would be extra special if you helped."

Whip Appeal Grilled Spiny Lobster Tails w/ *Bad Mamma Jamma* Rum Butter Sauce

Makes 2 servings

Prep Time: 15 minutes
Cooking Time: 15 minutes

Ingredients:

2 (1½ pound) spiny lobster tails

2 tablespoons butter, melted

½ cup Pyrat Rum

Instructions:

1. Lightly oil and preheat your grill for high heat.
2. Open the lobster tails lengthwise with kitchen shears; then split down the middle with a sharp knife.
3. Brush the flesh side with melted butter and lightly sprinkle the rum over each lobster tail.

4. Place shell side down on preheated grill and cook until the shell turns red—in about 5 minutes. Flip over and place the flesh side down and grill another 7-8 minutes. Brush with any remaining butter and grill for 1-2 minutes. Remove from the grill.
6. Lobster is done when the meat is white and not gray/opaque and the shell is bright red. Please, be cautious not to overcook.

Bad Mamma Jamma Rum Butter Sauce

Prep Time: 5 minutes
Cooking Time: 6-7 minutes

Ingredients:
½ cup butter
¼ vidalia onion, finely chopped
½ teaspoon white pepper
¼ teaspoon salt
¼ teaspoon cayenne pepper
3 tablespoons Pyrat Rum

Instructions:
1. In a saucepan over medium heat, add all 6 ingredients and cook until combined. Pour rum butter sauce over the lobster tails or serve as a dipping sauce on the side.

How Does It Feel Tropical Salad

Makes 2 servings

Prep Time: 15 minutes

Ingredients:

4 cups bite-sized pieces of romaine lettuce

¾ cup cherry tomatoes, halved

½ cup cucumbers, peeled and sliced

½ cup diced mango

½ cup shredded sharp cheddar cheese

1 small red onion, halved and thinly sliced

Instructions:

1. Wash the lettuce if it's not already done.
2. In a large bowl, combine all the ingredients and toss with the dressing of your choice.

Now that the salad is ready, the lobster tails should come off the grill. They smell delectable and I can't wait to devour them. One last thing to prepare—dessert—Somebody Loves You Baby Grilled Rum Cake. I'm so glad that I sent detailed instructions for all of the ingredients I would need for tonight's sexy dinner, including a local bakery's rum cake.

Somebody Loves You Baby **Grilled Rum Cake**

Makes 4 to 6 servings

Prep Time: 5 minutes

Cooking Time: 5 minutes

Ingredients:

1 (8-inch) Rum Cake from the local bakery

Instructions:

1. Brush the grill rack with vegetable oil.
2. Cut 4 slices of the rum cake about ½ inch each.
3. Place cake slices on grilling screen.
4. Grill cake uncovered about 4 to 6 inches from medium heat about 5 minutes, turning once, until golden brown.

My gentleman smells the aroma and can't stay away anymore. "Princess, everything smells divine and you did it so quickly. You never cease to amaze me. Thank you so much for cooking, even though we are on vacation." I invite him to handle the grilling of the few pieces of rum cake.

We decide to have dinner on our bedroom terrace. I prepare our plates and set the table, including dessert. We've decided to indulge in an island drink with our dinner—Seduction Planter's Punch.

The food is blessed and I must say that everything looks amazing! Before I have a chance to open my lobster tail, he has ripped his apart and grabbed a piece with his fingers. He comments that he's never tasted any lobster as good as this and that I should bottle the rum butter sauce. I finally get a chance to taste the lobster and it's so good. Like the saying goes, 'I really put my foot in it.' We engage in conversation, libations and a breathtaking view for an hour or so.

It's dessert time! The grilled rum cake is very moist, rich, flavorful and full of rum. What an amazing first night of our vacation? My gentleman turns to me and says he really appreciates everything that I've done to create such a fantastic first night of our vacation. And, he would like to show his appreciation by giving me a nice massage. I tingle all over at the thought of it. I excitedly respond, "That sounds great!"

I clean up our dinner dishes and head to the bedroom for

my massage. He has turned on some nice mellow music to set the mood. I remove my sexy apron and lay across the bed, as I am feeling relaxed and anxious all at the same time. My gentleman yells from the bathroom, "Are you ready?" I respond, "Yes I am!" Out of the bathroom he comes wearing absolutely nothing. I'm enjoying the view, but I was a little confused. I asked, "I thought I was getting the massage—so, why are you naked?" He just smiles.

Drink Suggestion(s)

***Seduction* Planter's Punch**

Makes 2 drinks

Ingredients:

4 oz. dark rum

2 oz. coconut rum

4 oz. orange juice

4 oz. pineapple juice

Dash grenadine

Orange slice and cherry for garnish

Instructions:

1. Combine the 2 juices and rums in a shaker with ice.
2. Shake well, and strain into an ice-filled glass.
3. Top with grenadine. Garnish with an orange slice and a maraschino cherry.

Music Suggestion(s)

Slow Jam—Usher

The Point of It All—Anthony Hamilton

So Beautiful—musiq Soulchild

Rocket Love—Stevie Wonder

Faded Pictures—Case featuring Joe

If You Love Me—Mint Condition

Angel of Mine—Monica

Fantasy #4
SUNDAY BRUNCH

It's Sunday morning and my gentleman and I attended the 7:30am morning service to receive our spiritual nourishment. Now, I am being dropped off at home, so my gentleman can finish a project from work, before coming back to my place for Brunch.

Our brunch menu has to be special, because we so enjoy this end of the week time together to relax and get prepared for the coming week. I've got it! How about one of my favorites—My First Love Red Velvet Waffles with a Breathe Again Cream Cheese Glaze and some Here I Stand Buttermilk Fried Chicken Tenders? He has been working so hard over the past week and I want to let him know that I care because he always looks out for me.

I definitely want everything to be hot when he gets here, so

I can take my time in preparing our meal, because it's now only 10:30am and he won't be over until 1. Now, let me get out of my church clothes, clean my face and put on a new glamorous look—smoky eyes, light mascara, pink frosted lip gloss and of course, a few mists of my French perfume, my sexy gladiator stilettos and most definitely, my sexy apron. Into the kitchen I go to prepare our delightful brunch. If nothing else, I will have the chicken battered and ready for frying, along with preparing the red velvet waffle batter. I have nice music playing and I love the light scent of the fresh flowers I've just placed on the table. Oh, I must not forget to chill a bottle or two of champagne for our Mama Mimosas.

Let's start with those My First Love Red Velvet Waffles.

My First Love **Red Velvet Waffles** *(Courtesy of cakeandallie.com)*

Makes 4 servings

Prep Time: 10 minutes

Cooking Time: 3-6 minutes per waffle [varies from one
                               waffle maker to another]

Ingredients:

¾ cup flour, minus 1½ tablespoons

1½ tablespoons cocoa powder

¼ cup cornstarch

½ teaspoon baking powder

¼ teaspoon baking soda

½ teaspoon salt

1½ teaspoons sugar

1 cup buttermilk

1/3 cup vegetable oil

1 large egg, beaten

¾ teaspoon vanilla extract

1½ teaspoons red food coloring

Instructions:

1. In a medium bowl, whisk together flour, cocoa, cornstarch, baking powder, baking soda, salt and sugar.
2. In a medium bowl, whisk together buttermilk, vegetable oil, egg, vanilla and red food coloring. Add dry ingredients to wet ingredients and whisk until mostly smooth, with a few lumps remaining. Let rest for 30 minutes.
3. Once you are ready to make the waffles, preheat the waffle maker. Pour the batter into the waffle maker, taking care not to overfill. Cook to manufacturer's instructions.
4. These waffles are best if eaten immediately, especially if you like your waffles crispy on the outside and fluffy on the inside.

Breathe Again Cream Cheese Glaze

Prep Time: 5 minutes

Cooking Time: 5-6 minutes

Ingredients:

1 (14 oz.) can sweetened condensed milk

4 ounces of cream cheese

¼ cup milk

½ teaspoon vanilla extract

Instructions:

1. In a saucepan over medium heat, add the sweetened condensed milk, cream cheese and milk; constantly stirring until the mixture combines smoothly. Remove from heat and add vanilla. Be careful not to burn this mixture.
2. Spread over your warm waffle, then top with your favorite syrup, as desired.

It's about 12:30pm, so I'll start frying the chicken tenders but I won't prepare the waffles until he has arrived.

Here I Stand **Buttermilk Fried Chicken Tenders**

Makes 2 servings

Prep Time: 40 minutes (includes marinating time)

Cooking Time: 10-11 minutes

Ingredients:

1½ pounds boneless, skinless chicken tenderloins

2½ cups vegetable oil (for cooking)

Buttermilk Marinade

2/3 cup buttermilk

1 teaspoon seasoned salt

Flour Mixture

2/3 cup all-purpose flour

1 teaspoon seasoned salt

2 teaspoons poultry seasoning

1 teaspoon black pepper

½ teaspoon paprika

¼ teaspoon cayenne pepper

Instructions:

1. Combine the chicken tenders with the buttermilk marinade; making sure the tenders are evenly coated.

2. Marinade for 30 minutes in refrigerator. For best results, marinate overnight.

3. Combine the flour, seasoned salt, poultry seasoning, black pepper, paprika and cayenne pepper in a large bowl.

4. Mix until well combined.
5. Coat each tender with the flour mixture and place on a plate.
6. Line another plate with a paper towel for draining the grease from the cooked tenders.
7. Add oil to a large skillet over high heat. Make sure the oil is hot before adding tenders. You can test by shaking a little bit of flour mixture into the oil. If it starts frying then the oil is ready.
8. Place chicken tenders into the hot oil.
9. Cook completely until golden brown on both sides—about 10-11 minutes.
10. Place the hot, cooked tenders on the plate lined with paper towels.

It's about 1:10 and my gentleman has arrived. I open the door and he greets me with a smile from ear to ear as he tells me that he could smell the chicken when he walked up to the door. I just laughed and told him that we are having My First Love Red Velvet Waffles with Breathe Again Cream Cheese Glaze and Here I Stand Buttermilk Fried Chicken Tenders. "Princess, I really needed this Brunch today, because I've had a very busy and stressful week, so let me thank you in advance." He says this as he kisses me gently on my neck.

"It's my pleasure!" I'm excited that he is here. Now come in and let me make you a Rock the Boat Mama Mimosa. You can sit back and relax while I prepare our waffles.

Drink Suggestion(s)

Rock the Boat Mama Mimosa *(Courtesy of About.com)*

Take your traditional Mimosa recipe and add a delicate splash of an orange liqueur topped with crushed raspberry ice that you make by pouring raspberry juice into an ice tray and letting it freeze. This mimosa is not called the Mama Mimosa for nothing!

Makes 2 drinks
Prep Time: 5 minutes

Ingredients:
½ gallon orange juice
750 ml bottle Champagne or Sparkling Wine
2 ounces orange liqueur
½ cup fresh raspberries

Instructions:
1. Pour the carton of chilled orange juice into a 3-quart pitcher and then add the full bottle of chilled Champagne or sparkling wine.
2. Next, add the 2 ounces of orange liqueur and stir with orange juice and Champagne until thoroughly mixed.

3. Just before serving, add the raspberry ice* to the pitcher and pour about 4 ounces of the mimosa mix into Champagne flutes. If you'd like to show off your special raspberry ice, simply pour the mimosa mix into regular wine glasses.

Raspberry ice. Crumble fresh raspberries and place the crumbles into narrow ice cube trays, fill with water and freeze. You can also use raspberry juice in the trays and freeze. Adds a very nice touch and great flavor to any Mimosa!

Back in the kitchen to prepare the waffles. And, since the batter is ready, all I need to do is get the waffle maker heated. It won't be long before the waffles are ready. While they are cooking, I'll add the chicken tenders to each plate.

Finally, the waffles are perfectly done—nice and crispy. Now, I'll drizzle some of the cream cheese glaze over each with just a little maple syrup. Both plates are now ready. My gentleman blesses the food. "Princess, you outdid yourself with today's brunch. I am so lucky to have you. Again, I thank you!" His smile was a great complement. We are engaged in conversation, great food, music playing and plenty of Rock the Boat Mama Mimosas. Before we know it, 2 hours had passed and we had discussed many great topics and enjoyed several mimosas. "Princess, you look so beautiful today." I blushed as I said, "Thanks, handsome!"

"Well, let me clear off the table so that you can have my undivided attention," I said. "While you're doing that, I'll be preparing a special surprise for you." He looked excited to do something for me. I was excited and said, "Really?"

A few minutes later he called out from the other room. "Princess, please grab your glass of mimosa and come join me?" "Where are you?" I said as my voice elevated because I was anxious, nervous and excited all at the same time. "Just follow my voice." The anticipation made me feel warm all over and then I entered the bathroom. Oh, what a beautiful surprise! "Is that my favorite milk bath with fresh rose petals?" I was overwhelmed with joy. "Yes, and your favorite scented candles," he said proudly.

He helped me remove my stilettos, then I took my time and removed my apron. I eased down into the warm sensation and said, "Oh, this milk bath feels so good . . . Thank you, my dear gentleman." Looking pleased he responded, "Absolutely."

Music Suggestion(s)

Groove Me—Guy

So Anxious—Ginuwine

There'll Never Be—Switch

Never Gonna Let You Go—Faith Evans

Someone to Love—Jon B

Don't Rush—Silk

Best of My Love—The Emotions

Fantasy #5
BREAKFAST IN BED

It's Saturday morning and what a busy week I've had? Back to back meetings, conference calls and client dinners—every day. Believe it or not, I've not had a chance to see my gentlemen at all this week, but I'm about to change that. I am going to make him breakfast in bed this morning. I have a new recipe—my Slow Jam Pancake Lasagna that I am going to serve him with a Red Light Special Peach Bellini. It's 7:00am, so it's time for me to get up, shower and grab all the ingredients from my pantry and fridge. Let's see, I'll need flour, syrup, eggs, shredded cheddar cheese, sausage and bacon . . . and let's not forget the peaches for our special drink.

Time to shower, apply my flawless makeup and put on something tantalizing. Today is a good day to put on one of my beautiful red sundresses, my strappy kitten-heeled sandals with the jewel embellishment, some French perfume, and I can never forget my red lipstick. When my gentleman sees me, he is going to melt. Groceries . . .check, my sexy apron . . .check, and my keys . . .check, now off to my gentleman's house I go.

He lives only 20 minutes away. I arrive at his home, drop the groceries in the kitchen and head straight to the bedroom. "Good morning, my dear gentleman." He turned to greet me as I gently rubbed his leg. "Princess, you look beautiful and I love to see you in red." I smiled. "I missed you and wanted to serve you breakfast in bed. So please, go back to sleep and I will wake you when everything is ready."

I head to the bathroom and change into my sexy apron and now to the kitchen. I know my gentleman is going to love the Slow Jam Pancake Lasagna and his refreshing Red Light Special Peach Bellini.

Slow Jam Pancake Lasagna *(Courtesy of Eric Greenspan)*

Makes 6 servings

Prep Time: 45 minutes

Cooking Time: 1 hour

Ingredients:

Batter

1½ cups buttermilk

¼ cup milk

2½ tablespoons butter, melted, plus more for skillet

2 small eggs

1½ cups all-purpose flour

2 tablespoons white granulated sugar

1½ teaspoons baking powder

¾ teaspoons baking soda

Instructions:

1. Preheat the oven to 375 degrees F.
2. Mix the buttermilk, milk, melted butter and eggs in a large mixing bowl. In a separate bowl, mix the flour, white sugar, baking powder and baking soda. Slowly add the dry mix into the wet mix with a whisk until incorporated.
3. In a buttered large skillet, ladle 4 ounces (½ cup) of the batter. Brown each side, flipping when bottom is browned and the top is beginning to bubble. Remove the pancake and repeat cooking instructions until all the batter is done. Square off the edges of each pancake and set aside.

Bacon and Sausage

15 strips bacon

15 links breakfast sausage

¼ cup fresh sage, chopped

Instructions:

1. Place a grill rack over a baking tray. Line the rack with the bacon strips and bake until crispy—about 15 minutes. Reserve the rendered oil in a large saucepot.
2. Line a baking tray with the sausage links and bake until cooked thoroughly—about 15 minutes. Chop the sausage finely, place in a bowl, add the chopped sage and mix.

Eggs

12 eggs

Butter, for the skillet

¼ cup heavy cream

Instructions:

1. Whisk the eggs until smooth. Cook in a buttered large skillet over medium heat until cooked completely and are light and fluffy. Place in a blender and add enough cream until blended smoothly.
2. Remove and let cool.

Maple Béchamel

¼ cup butter

¼ cup all-purpose flour

1 quart heavy cream

2 cups maple syrup

Butter, for greasing

1 pound shredded cheddar cheese

½ cup maple syrup

Instructions:

1. Add the butter and flour to the reserved bacon fat in the large saucepan and make a roux. Add the cream and maple syrup and cook over low heat, stirring until thickened—about 20 minutes. The sauce should have the consistency of gravy.

To assemble:

1. Butter a casserole dish, then line the bottom with a single layer of pancakes.
2. Lightly spread the béchamel over the pancakes until covered.
3. Place the chopped sausage on top of the pancakes, spreading evenly until covered.
4. Spoon half the egg mixture over the sausage and spread until evenly dispersed.
5. Add another layer of the béchamel, and then add a layer of the shredded cheddar cheese.
6. Repeat the layering by adding another layer of pancakes, then béchamel, then bacon strips, béchamel again, then eggs and finish with a liberal covering of cheese.

7. Bake until the cheese has melted on top and begun to get crispy—about 10 minutes.
8. Remove from the oven and let cool. Then cut lasagna into even portions.
9. Place a portion of lasagna on a plate and spoon the syrup over the top to taste.

Note: This recipe makes a lot of servings, but you can place the leftovers in freezer bags and save up to 1 month. Allow it to thaw then reheat in the oven at low heat for about 20 minutes.

The aroma has caused my gentleman to get out of the bed and come into the kitchen to see exactly what I'm cooking. I tell him, "It's my Slow Jam Pancake Lasagna." "Princess, I can't wait!" "Go get back in the bed and I will have your breakfast ready in a few minutes." I playfully push him towards the door. "Princess, you are one of a kind! Thank God for you!" He leaves to get back in bed.

Now, I can focus on the Red Light Special Peach Bellini before I prepare my gentleman's tray.

Drink Suggestion(s)

Red Light Special Peach Bellini *(Adapted from food.com)*
Makes 4 servings
Prep Time: 15 minutes

Ingredients:
6 ounces Moscato
1 ounce Peach Schnapps, to taste
½ cup frozen peaches, sliced
Ice

Instructions:
1. Add a few frozen peach slices and the schnapps to the blender and puree. The mixture should be taking on a slushy type texture.
2. Taste and add more peach schnapps or peaches, as needed. Add ice and continue to blend until a nice frozen texture is acquired. Pour into Champagne flutes and garnish with a peach slice.

Breakfast is finally ready! Let's start with the fun part of preparing my gentleman's tray. I've cut a generous piece of the pancake lasagna and drizzled a little of the maple béchamel sauce all over the top, poured him a Peach Bellini, grabbed today's local newspaper, folded a linen napkin and carefully placed the flatware. I will definitely get some brownie points for this breakfast! I slowly walk upstairs to my gentleman's bedroom. I enter the room to find him sitting up in his bed with the biggest smile on his face.

"Princess, you are the sweetest woman I have ever met. And, you excite me so much with your wonderful food. I can truly taste the love in all of your dishes." His words are touching. "My dear gentleman, you are so deserving of it and thanks for always looking out for me and taking care of things when I need you. This is just a small token of my appreciation for all that you do!"

"Princess, where is your plate?" He wondered. "I'll eat later because I wanted to feed you breakfast first." Surprised, he said, "You're going to feed me? Wow, I know I've died and gone to heaven." I sit on the edge of the bed and bless the food. Now, I cut small pieces of the lasagna and slowly feed my gentleman. "Princess, this lasagna is so good and filling. And my Bellini is divine. However, I cannot sit here and allow you to continue feeding me, when I know that you haven't eaten and you've spent a few hours preparing my breakfast.

Come get in the bed." He gestures for me to come close as he serves me his remaining pancake lasagna and bellini. And he wasn't lying . . .the pancake lasagna is so scrumptious.

I take the tray back to the kitchen, turn on some nice music and clean up all the dirty dishes. Of course, my gentleman is still lying in the bed—probably asleep. After cleaning up the kitchen, I am dancing to some nice slow music—in my own world—when out of nowhere my gentleman appears and evidently he had been watching me dance. He picks me up in his strong arms and takes me to the bedroom and places me gently on the bed.

"Princess, I'm hungry again." His voice sounded playful and sexy. "My dear gentleman, I noticed that you grabbed some of the maple béchamel sauce from the kitchen, but, where is the pancake lasagna? What are you going to eat and what are you going to do with the béchamel sauce?"

"Princess, please just lay back and relax!"

How to get a man . . .

Ready or Not—After 7

My First, My Last, My Everything—Barry White

Loving You—Minnie Ripperton

My Endless Love—Diana Ross & Lionel Richie

Your Body's Callin'—R. Kelly

Pretty Brown Eyes—Mint Condition

Never Gonna Let You Go—Faith Evans

Fantasy #6
VALENTINE'S DAY

It's Friday, February 14th—Valentine's Day. I am actually in the office today to meet with my staff for our weekly management team meeting. It's about 10:30am and my secretary has just buzzed me to tell me that I have a visitor. A Visitor? How sweet! My wonderful gentleman has surprised me at my office with 6 dozen assorted colored, long stemmed roses. "Princess, these are for you, because you are so special to me and I want you to know it. And, I'll have another gift for you tonight at dinner."

"Oh My God, this is the sweetest thing. Thank you so much!" I can't hold back the tears. "Princess, don't cry!" He's so understanding. "I'm just happy and these are tears of joy!" He puts his hand under my chin and gently raises my head and looks me in the eyes. "Well, I'll let you get back to work. I can't wait to see you for dinner at your house tonight." I'm so excited, but I've got to get myself together for my meeting and of course, my staff, who were watching the moment, are overjoyed for me as well. They have told me on multiple occasions that I have a good man, but they didn't have to tell me, because I already knew. That's why I don't mind cooking nice meals for him and taking care of him. Speaking of which, I've decided that for tonight's dinner I will prepare my Use Your Heart Lobster Mac & Cheese and for dessert my Come Get To This Chocolate Dipped Strawberries.

I just finished my meeting, so I can leave the office now. En route to my house, I stopped by the florist to pick up a few bags of fresh rose petals and now to the grocery store to grab the ingredients for our sexy and delicious dinner.

I've finally made it home—and I'm still in shock about the beautiful flowers my handsome gentleman delivered to me this morning. I definitely want to make sure that our dinner is spectacular! It's 3:45pm and he will be here at 7pm, so I have some time to focus on our dinner and making myself look extra sexy. First things first, I need a nice, hot bath with some of my scented bubble bath. This bubble bath is so relaxing! Thirty minutes have passed and I am still soaking. I think it's time for me to get out and get my glam together. I've dried off, applied some lotion, flawless makeup with my red lipstick, some body glitter, a red rose in my hair, my sexy apron and a pair of my sexy red, strappy stilettos. My gentleman is going to be all smiles and I'm not mad at him!

I noticed that it's 5:30pm, time to start preparing dinner. So, I begin to prepare the *Use Your Heart* Lobster Mac & Cheese, even though I won't bake it until right before he arrives.

Use Your Heart Lobster Mac & Cheese

Makes 4 to 6 servings

Prep Time: 20 minutes

Cooking Time: 30 minutes

Ingredients:

1 box elbow macaroni

1 teaspoon extra virgin olive oil

2 cups heavy whipping cream

1 stick of butter, plus 3 tablespoons

1½ cups Gruyère cheese

½ cup sharp cheddar cheese

½ pepper jack cheese

1 teaspoon salt

½ teaspoon pepper

2 eggs

2 pounds lobster meat, chopped

1 ½ cups Ritz crackers, crushed

[I use 2 pounds of lobster, because I love to taste the lobster in every bite, but you can use 1 pound for this recipe—and it's cost effective.]

Instructions:

1. Preheat oven to 375 degrees F.
2. Drizzle oil into a large pot of boiling salted water. Add the pasta and cook according to the directions on the package, 6 to 8 minutes. Drain well.
3. Meanwhile, heat the heavy whipping cream in a saucepan; add butter. Cook over low heat for 4 to 5 minutes, stirring with a whisk. Remove from heat, and then add the Gruyère, cheddar and pepper jack cheeses, salt and pepper.
4. Crack the eggs in a small bowl; then pour in a ½ cup of the hot cheese sauce while slowly whisking for a few moments. Pour this mixture back into the saucepan. Now what you've just done is called egg tempering. As defined by tablespoon.com, tempering is when you add a hot liquid to an egg mixture. The goal is to slowly bring up the temperature of the eggs without scrambling them.
4. Add the cooked macaroni and lobster to the cheese mixture; stir well. Place the mixture in a greased casserole dish.

5. Melt the remaining 3 tablespoons of butter, combine with the crushed Ritz crackers and sprinkle on the top of macaroni.
6. Bake for 30 to 35 minutes, or until the sauce is bubbly and the macaroni is browned on the top.

Now, I'll work on dessert—the Come Get To This Chocolate Dipped Strawberries.

Tempt Your Senses

Chocolate Who doesn't know about chocolate as an aphrodisiac food? On Valentine's Day, the day to express your love, more chocolate is sold than at any other time during the year. Chocolate is given during the holidays, for anniversaries and just to say "I love you." Chocolate contains a stimulant called phenyl ethylamine, which gives you a sense of well-being and excitement similar to the natural high that endorphins gives us. Researchers believe that chocolate contains chemicals that affect neurotransmitters in the brain, and a substance related to caffeine called theobromine. There are more antioxidants in chocolate than in red wine. Combining the two can be the secret to passion.
Courtesy of www.fuelthemind.com

Come Get To This Chocolate Dipped Strawberries

Makes 14 strawberries

Prep Time: 10 minutes

Cooking Time: 10 minutes

Cooling Time: 30 minutes

Ingredients:

½ cup heavy whipping cream

1 cup milk chocolate chip morsels

2 tablespoons butter, room temperature

1 pound fresh strawberries with stems/leaves (about 14)

Instructions:

1. Rinse the strawberries and pat dry with a paper towel.
2. In a small saucepan, heat heavy whipping cream on medium heat for 10 minutes. Bring to a simmer.
3. Pour warm cream mixture over milk chocolate chip morsels. Let set for 1 minute.
4. Whisk cream and chocolate chip morsels until completely incorporated.
5. Add butter and mix until completely smooth.
6. Line a baking sheet with parchment paper.
7. Insert toothpicks into the tops of the strawberries.
8. Holding them by the toothpicks, dip the strawberries into the chocolate mixture until completely covered, gently shaking off any excess.
9. Place on parchment paper and continue dipping the remaining strawberries.

10. Allow the chocolate to set on the strawberries, about 30 minutes in the refrigerator, before serving. You can also dip them into nuts, candy or any of your favorite toppings, etc.

So, while the strawberries are setting, I will prepare my place for our romantic Valentine's Day rendezvous. First, I'm lighting some candles throughout the entire house. I have some of my favorite slow, sexy music playing throughout the space. I've sprinkled the rose petals that I bought earlier throughout the house creating a trail that leads to the bedroom. My final step is to make a heart of roses on the bed. The mood is definitely set for a romantic evening with my gentleman.

My phone rings and it's my gentleman calling to let me know that he is headed to my house. He really has me feeling excited and loved right now! He is such a considerate, affectionate, caring, romantic, God fearing, handsome and hardworking, accomplished man. He's such a blessing to me!

Now, let me dash back into the kitchen to put my special mac and cheese into the oven. I want it to be nice and hot when my gentleman arrives.

Prompt as always, my gentleman has arrived. Oh my goodness. He's bearing another 6 dozen roses and all I can do is smile. "Princess, these are for you. You don't realize how special you are to me and that I truly love you?" All I can say is, "Wow!" "Don't cry princess!" He pulls my hand and brings me close to his chest. "I've never met a man like you, but I am so thankful for you." I grab several vases to display my beautiful, assorted colored roses throughout the house and the flowers smell amazing.

"Princess, what is that smell?" "It's my Use Your Heart Lobster Mac and Cheese." He licks his lips and says, "I can't wait!" "Well, you don't have to, but all I need to do is to prepare our plates." While I prepare our plates, my gentleman pours the You're The One Lolailo Sangria in our glasses. The food is blessed and we begin to indulge in our Valentine's Day dinner and I can't imagine being anywhere else right now. We converse, while enjoying the Sangria, the food and each other's company. "Princess, I've been waiting for this moment all day!" He smiles at me. "My dear gentleman, so have I!"

"This Lobster Mac and Cheese is so good that I'm going to call my mother to tell her all about it. I think I need a second helping, because I'm addicted to the taste." "I'll grab some more for you." As I head to the kitchen to put another serving of the mac and cheese on his plate, he fills our glasses with more Sangria. Two hours have passed and we are still enjoying our dinner.

"My dear gentleman, don't get too full because I've prepared Come Get To This Chocolate Dipped Strawberries. I grab some of the strawberries and place them in one of my pretty martini glasses. I walk over to my gentleman's chair and sit on the edge of it and begin feeding him the strawberries. "Princess, they are divine, but I want you to have some too." He grabs a strawberry from the martini glass and slowly brings it to my mouth as I open wide to enjoy the succulent treat! Now that we are both full, I place the few dishes in the dishwasher, so that I can give him my undivided attention.

"My dear gentleman, I have a surprise for you . . . Now close your eyes and just hold my hand. I walk him down the hallway to the opening of my bedroom. You can open your eyes now." He looks around the room with delight. "Princess, you did this for me? You had time to make a heart out of roses and you have roses leading down the hallway. You are so creative! This has been the best Valentine's Day—ever! But, you know I still have a taste for something sweet!"

"Would you like for me to make some more strawberries?" "No, because I have another gift for you." "Wow, this box is so beautifully wrapped! I wonder what this could be? I open the box to find a sexy pair of chocolate thongs. I can barely get them on before my gentleman takes a bite. "Princess, this chocolate tastes exquisite! I think its Belgian!" I respond, "Ooh La La!"

Tempt Your Senses

Raspberries and strawberries These are perfect aphrodisiac foods to hand feed your lover. They are red, which is the color associated with love and passion, and are high in vitamin C. *Courtesy of www.fuelthemind.com*

You're The One Lolailo Sangria*

Makes 4 to 6 drinks

Prep Time: 10 minutes

Ingredients:

1 orange, sliced

1 apple, sliced

1 peach, sliced

1 lemon, sliced

1 lime, sliced

Note: Lolailo Sangria is the brand name and can be purchased at most beverage/liquor retailers.

Instructions:

1. Pour the bottle of Sangria into a pitcher.
2. Add sliced fruit, place into the refrigerator to chill before serving.

My First Love—Avant

My Body—LSG

You Know What's Up—Darnell Jones featuring Lisa "Lefteye" Lopes

Ready For Love—India Arie

Say Yes—Floetry

Love Of My Life—Brian McKnight

You Are My Lady—Freddie Jackson

Fantasy #7
DATE NIGHT

Thank God's it's Friday! It's the end of the week and Date Night for me and my gentleman. We haven't had Date Night in about 2 months, so I'm looking forward to it. We normally meet at each other's home and have a picnic right in the living room floor. We've decided to meet at my house tonight…With that being said, I need to create tonight's menu. He loves my How Many Ways Steak with Roasted Garlic Butter, How Deep is Your Love Loaded Baked Potatoes, Differences Caesar Salad and for dessert—Piece of My Love Godiva Nut Lovers Truffle Flight and Fresh Green & Purple Grapes.

It's 5pm and dinner will be ready at 7pm. And, since it's a cold winter night, we can have our picnic in front of the fireplace. How romantic? I hope my gentleman can handle our evening.

because I can't wait to see him...he really excites me! Since I have some time, let me gather everything that's needed for our romantic picnic. Let's see, I need my luxurious blanket, some scented candles and some nice, soft music. Now that I have everything in order, let me take a relaxing bubble bath.

While soaking, I am thinking about the many romantic times that I've spent with my gentleman... and I must say that this man always puts a smile on my face. I thank God for placing such a beautiful soul on this earth, and more specifically, for putting him in my life. I know that he is a blessing!

I've been soaking for 30 minutes, so I think it's time to get out. I dry off; apply some scented lotion and a few squirts of French perfume. I've also applied my flawless makeup, to include my red, lip gloss that accentuates my full lips, my sexy apron and a pair of sexy, black heeled bedroom slippers with fur. It's now 6pm and he will be here in 1 hour, so I dash into the kitchen to get started with tonight's meal.

How Many Ways Steak with Roasted Garlic Butter

Makes 2 servings

Prep Time: 45 minutes

Cooking Time: 6–25 minutes *(depending on personal preference – rare to well done)*

Ingredients:

2 (16 oz) rib eye steaks

1 stick butter, softened

2 tablespoons roasted garlic, minced

1 teaspoon Italian seasoning

1 teaspoon steak seasoning

Pinch of salt and pepper

Instructions:

1. Preheat oven to 475 degrees F.
2. Sprinkle salt and pepper on each steak (front and back).
3. Mix softened butter, roasted garlic, Italian and steak seasonings in a small bowl. Generously spread butter mixture over the front and back of steaks.
4. Place steaks in heavy roasting pan and cook to your preference, then remove from the oven. *Note: The cooking time varies based on: the cooking temperature, size, thickness and doneness of the steak.* To test the doneness, insert a meat thermometer into the center of the thickest part of the steak. Rare= 120 degrees; Medium Rare= 126 degrees; Medium= 135 degrees; Medium Well= 145 degrees; Well Done= 150 degrees.

5. If you have any of the remaining butter mixture—now is the perfect time to spread a little more, along with any pan drippings.
6. Allow the steaks to rest for a few minutes before serving.

Roasted Garlic Recipe
Makes 10 to 12 teaspoons
Prep Time: 5 minutes
Cooking Time: 40-45 minutes

Ingredients:
1 whole medium size garlic bulb
1- 2 teaspoons extra virgin olive oil
Note: Each garlic bulb yields 10-12 garlic cloves; 1-2 teaspoons of olive oil is needed per bulb; each garlic head/clove yields 1-1½ teaspoons. Cooking time will vary based on the size of the garlic bulb.

Instructions:
1. Preheat oven to 400 degrees F.
2. Peel away the outer layers of skin of the garlic bulb, leaving the skins of the individual cloves intact.
3. Using a sharp knife, cut off the pointed ends of the garlic bulbs, which will expose the individual cloves.
4. Place the garlic bulb on a sheet of aluminum foil and drizzle olive oil over the garlic cloves until well coated. Gather the sides of the foil making a pouch.

5. Bake for 40-45 minutes, until the garlic is very soft.

6. Open the pouch and allow the garlic to cool before trying to handle. Each garlic clove will slide right out.

Note: Remember each garlic bulb yields 10-12 garlic cloves. So if you only require a few cloves, you can also separate the quantity that's needed from the bulb; remove the paper like skin; cut off the pointed ends and follow Steps 4 through 6. However, with smaller quantities, you should start checking the cloves after 10 minutes to make sure that you do not burn them. Larger bulbs will take more time. And remember, any extra garlic can be added to butter and parsley, then spread across bread slices to make amazing garlic bread.

How Deep Is Your Love Loaded Baked Potato

Makes 2 servings

Prep Time: 5 minutes

Cooking Time: 13 minutes

Ingredients:

2 large Russet potatoes

Toppings Per Potato

1 tablespoon butter or margarine

2 tablespoons shredded sharp cheddar cheese

1 tablespoon Hormel real crumbled bacon

2 tablespoons sour cream

Salt and Pepper to taste

Instructions:

1. Wash and scrub each potato; prick each several times with a fork. Place on a microwavable plate.
2. Microwave for 6 minutes. Turnover and cook for another 6 minutes. Remove from the microwave and cut in half lengthwise. Mash the inside of each potato, using a fork or spoon.
3. Add butter, salt, pepper and cheese to each potato. Place in the microwave for 1 minute to melt the cheese.
4. Top with bacon and sour cream. Serve hot.

Differences Caesar Salad

Makes 2 servings

Prep Time: 10 – 15 minutes

Ingredients:

3 cups bite-sized pieces of romaine lettuce

½ cup croutons

8 grape tomatoes, halved

¼ cup Parmesan cheese, grated

Caesar Dressing

Instructions:

1. Toss lettuce with desired Caesar dressing.
2. Add croutons, tomatoes and Parmesan cheese.
3. Refrigerate and keep chilled until ready to serve.

Piece of My Love Godiva Nut Lovers Truffles and Fresh Seedless Green and Purple Grapes
Makes 2 servings
Prep time: 10 minutes

Ingredients:
1 box – Godiva Nut Lovers Truffle Flight – 6 pieces – Salted Almond, Hazelnut Crunch, Pecan Caramel, Butterscotch Walnut, Maple Walnut and Pistachio
1 bunch seedless Green Grapes
1 bunch seedless Purple Grapes

Instructions:
1. Rinse grapes and pat dry with a paper towel. Place on silver platter and add box of chocolate truffles.
2. Refrigerate until ready to serve.

It's 7:05pm and my gentleman has arrived. I greet and welcome him at the door with a nice hug and of course, he comes bearing a bouquet of tropical flowers. "Princess, you look beautiful as ever." The mere sound of his voice makes me melt. "Thanks my dear gentleman for the compliment and the flowers, as they are beautiful and smell amazing." He responds, "the aroma in your kitchen is amazing. Princess, what are we having tonight?" "We're having How Many Ways

Steak with Roasted Garlic Butter, How Deep is Your Love Loaded Baked Potatoes, Differences Caesar Salad and for Dessert—a platter filled with Piece of My Love Godiva Nut Lovers Truffles with Fresh Green and Purple Grapes."

"Princess, I can't believe you prepared this succulent meal for our picnic. "So, where are we eating our dinner tonight?" "Well, my dear gentleman, I think it's only fitting to have our picnic close to the fireplace on this cool evening. And, I've taken the liberty of placing the blanket, candles and the picnic basket, which contains our plates and flatware that will be used for tonight, right by the fireplace." I look over at my gentleman and he is all smiles…and that makes me feel so good.

While I prepare our plates, I ask my dear gentleman to turn on the music, light the candles and pour us each a glass of Merlot. "Princess, it's my pleasure and is the least that I can do." The plates are ready and I've cut the steak in pieces since we are dining in the living room on the floor—just to make things easier for the both of us. We are now cozy in front of the fireplace in the living room…the soft music is playing in the background. We hold hands and my gentleman blesses our food. He gushes, "I don't know where to start, as it all looks so good. And, princess thanks for cutting up the steak for me, as it really makes it easier for me to enjoy our date night dinner." "You're welcome!" We are enjoying our dinner, the wine, music, ambiance and our conversation. "Oh my, my, my, this steak is so tender that it's melting in my mouth like butter. I don't even need any steak sauce!" His excitement is like a bolt of lightning that makes me tingle. I smile and continue to enjoy our picnic. Out of nowhere, my gentleman grabs my hand and asks me to dance...and of course, I oblige.

We start dancing and he begins to sing Love's Holiday by Earth, Wind & Fire to me. Since we started dating, he has never sang to me and I'm not sure what's happening right now, but I'm loving it. He whispers in my ear, I love you Princess and I am dedicating this song to you and this is exactly how I feel about you. I am enjoying this special moment and being held by my gentleman's strong arms...Thank you God!

The song is over, but we continue to gaze into each other's eyes. "Princess, thanks for the dance" I reply, "my pleasure!"

We sit back down onto our blanket and have decided that we are ready for dessert. I grab our plates, clean them very quickly and pull out our dessert platter. "So, my dear gentleman, for dessert—we are having some wonderful chocolate truffles with green and purple seedless grapes. I figured since we were having such a heavy meal, that I would go light on dessert. And here's a nice bottle of Riesling to go along with the chocolate and grapes."

I grab a few of the grapes and start to feed my gentleman and he responds that they are so sweet and succulent. I then feed him one of the decadent Godiva truffles and he is in heaven. He offers to feed me a few and a truffle and the flavors explode in my mouth. "My dear princess, I have an idea." I reply, "what's the idea?" He responds, "I'll show you." So he places the grapes and truffles precisely in a row on the platter and only uses his mouth (no hands) to devour the remaining dessert. Who knew I could fit so perfectly on this platter? I'm in Heaven!

Drink Suggestion(s)

Nice bottle or 2 of Merlot – Meal

Bottle of Riesling – Dessert

Music Suggestion(s)

The Finest—S.O.S. Band

With You—Tony Terry

Strip For You—R. Kelly

The Closer I Get to You—Luther Vandross and Beyoncé

Love's Holiday—Earth, Wind & Fire

Always In My Heart—Tevin Campbell

Read Your Mind—Avant

Tempt Your Senses

Wine Wine relaxes our inhibitions and stimulates our senses. The actual drinking of wine can be an erotic experience. Moderate amounts of wine are believed to arouse or leave a momentary flush in your face, but excessive alcohol will make you drowsy. *Courtesy of www.fuelthemind.com*

Fantasy #8
BUSINESS DINNER

It's Friday evening and tomorrow is my gentleman's business dinner. Since he was recently promoted to Executive Vice President at his pharmaceutical company, he has decided to have dinner at his home with the executives from the office. Not only that, but yours truly will be preparing this special dinner. I will have an opportunity to meet my gentleman's colleagues and they will have an opportunity to taste my cuisine and meet me, as well. This is going to be an event to remember.

So, I've decided to prepare a French inspired meal. Let's Stay Together Coq Au Vin served over I'm Bossy Red Skinned Mashed Potatoes with Cheese, Forever My Lady French Cut String Beans with Almonds and for Dessert—The Point of It All Vanilla Crème Brulee and Assorted Sorbets.

Saturday has arrived and dinner is scheduled for 8pm. My gentleman is going to pick me up from home at 2pm, so that he can help me grab all of the needed ingredients. And, since this is a business dinner and as much as he loves to see me in my sexy apron, I will not be able to wear it today. So, into the closet I go to find a nice, conservative sexy dress. I have a nice colorful knee-length A-line dress that I will pair with some sexy stilettos. This will be perfect for this evening's festivities. Well, let me start my ritual with a nice, soaking bubble bath. While bathing, I am listening to some nice mellow music and just thinking about how wonderful tonight will be and how important it is to my gentleman. All I can do is smile!

After 30 minutes of soaking, I dry off and give myself a nice facial. The facial is done and now, let's apply my flawless makeup with a natural lip gloss; my hair is pinned up and I'm wearing a pair of diamond stud earrings and matching necklace; a few squirts of my French perfume and now I'm ready. I have a completely different look today—conservative, but definitely sexy.

My gentleman is here! I race to the door to greet him with

a kiss. "Good afternoon, my dear gentleman." He responds, "Princess you are absolutely beautiful!" I reply, "Thank you!" Now we head to the kitchen to grab all the ingredients for this evening's dinner. I took the liberty of bagging everything before I bathed. He grabs all the bags and places them in the car. I grab my purse and off to his house we go. However, because of time constraints I will not have time to prepare dessert, so we are going to stop at the French bakery to pick up the Vanilla Crème Brulee and then make another stop by the ice cream parlor to pick up some assorted sorbets.

We've made it to my gentleman's home and I dash to the powder room. While I'm washing my hands, my gentleman is unpacking the groceries in efforts of helping me. He then opens a bottle of champagne and pours me a glass. The first thing I need to do is focus on preparing the plate settings on the formal dining room table, only adding the pieces that are applicable to the food that is being served. The beautiful cream linen tablecloth has been placed so nicely on the table and let's not forget the matching napkins with beaded napkin rings. I've also added a beautiful bouquet of flowers in the center of the table. Lastly, the 10 place settings have been added and I must say the table is absolutely breathtaking, with its beautiful fine china, crystal stemware and silver flatware. In case I didn't mention it earlier, there are 4 executives with their guests attending this evening's dinner, along with my gentleman and me—for a total of 10!

Etiquette Place Setting for Formal Dinner
(Courtesy of www.ehow.com)
For a formal dinner, the dinner plate should be set in the center of the cutlery, between the knives and forks, with the soup bowl set on top of the plate. Forks are always placed to the left of the dinner plate, and knives always go to the right. If a soup spoon is needed, that should also be placed to the right. There are three types of forks required: the salad fork should be placed to the furthest left, followed by the dinner fork in the center and the dessert fork on the right. The napkin should be folded and placed to the left of the forks.

On the right of the plate, the dinner knife is placed to the immediate right of the plate, with the teaspoon to the right, followed by the soup spoon. A smaller side plate should be set above the forks, with small butter knife laid across the plate. The glassware should be set above the knives, with the water glass to the furthest left, followed by the red wine glass and then the white wine glass.

Now on to preparing dinner. Let's start my Let's Stay Together Coq Au Vin.

Let's Stay Together Coq Au Vin

Makes 12 servings

Prep Time: 45 minutes

Cooking Time: 2 hours 15 minutes

Ingredients:

1 pound bacon slices, cut into 1 inch pieces

2 whole chicken fryers, each cut into 8 pieces, skin on

Salt & pepper to taste

2 large yellow onions, chopped

4 cups diced carrots, cut into 1 inch pieces

2 (8.5 oz.) jars Bella Sun Luci sun dried tomatoes

10 roasted garlic cloves*

4 cups chicken stock

4 cups red wine (burgundy, merlot or pinot noir)

A few bay leaves

Several fresh thyme sprigs

4 tablespoons butter

4 tablespoons flour

Note: Roasted garlic recipe included in Fantasy #7—Date Night.

Instructions:

1. Preheat oven to 350 degrees F.
2. Brown bacon on medium heat in a dutch oven (large enough to accommodate all the chicken pieces).
3. Remove the bacon with a slotted spoon and set aside.
4. Season chicken with salt and pepper on both sides.
5. Depending on the amount of chicken to be cooked, you

may have to cook in batches. Add the 1st batch of chicken to the bacon fat in the dutch oven. Cook 5-6 minutes on each side until the skin is golden brown and crispy. Remove chicken from dutch oven and set aside. Cook the next batch of chicken and remove and set aside with the other browned chicken.

6. Add the chopped onions, carrots, sun-dried tomatoes and garlic to the dutch oven.
7. Add chicken stock.
8. Add wine.
9. Add cooked bacon and stir thoroughly.
10. Add bay leaves and thyme sprigs.
11. Cover and place in oven for 1½ hours.
12. Remove from oven and discard the bay leaves and thyme sprigs.
13. Place dutch oven over medium heat.
14. Mix butter and flour, until it forms a paste. Stir in the paste and simmer for 20 minutes, as this will thicken the sauce.
15. Serve with I'm Bossy Red Skinned Mashed Potatoes with Cheese (recipe included in Fantasy #1—His Big Promotion). This dish can also be served over egg noodles.

Note: This recipe can be scaled down for fewer servings.

The kitchen has an amazing food aroma and my gentleman and I have been enjoying the fragrance and the champagne. Now let's make my Forever My Lady French Cut String Beans with Almonds.

Forever My Lady French Cut String Beans with Almonds

Makes 10 to 12 servings

Prep Time: 5 minutes

Cooking Time: 40-45 minutes

Ingredients:

3 (16 oz.) bags french cut string beans, frozen

2½ cups water

3 teaspoons salt

2 teaspoons pepper

2½ teaspoons sugar

4 tablespoons butter

1 cup slivered almonds, roasted

Instructions:

1. Place string beans in large saucepan, add water and cook on high heat for 15 minutes (covered). Drain.
2. Add salt, pepper, sugar and butter; stir well and continue to cook for another 25 to 30 minutes.
3. In a skillet, add almonds. As they start to heat, turn them often. When they start to turn brown, they are ready. Please pay attention to the almonds to ensure that they don't burn. Remove from heat.
4. Add to string bean mixture.

Dinner is ready and it's 7:30pm. Now, I'll head to the powder room to freshen up my makeup and to add a few squirts of French perfume (since I've been cooking for a few hours). This dinner is really going to impress my gentleman's colleagues and he is so excited about having his first business dinner. It's 7:45pm and the guests have started to arrive. The CEO and his wife arrive first, so obviously my gentleman introduces me and now we offer them a glass of French champagne and they oblige. I've decided to place the food on the table and before we know it, the remaining guests have arrived, including the Chairman of the Board, his wife, the Vice President and his guest. The proper introductions are being made and everyone is complimenting us on the food aroma coming from the kitchen...We all head to the formal dining room and are seated, with my gentleman at one end of the table and me at the other.

The food is blessed and everyone is making their plates and cannot believe what they are seeing—Coq Au Vin. While the plates are being made, the glasses are being filled with an assortment of French libations, including Champagne, Bordeaux, and a choice of Burgundy or Condrieu.

Everyone is complimenting me on the flavorful food and that they'd not had anything as good since they last visited their favorite French restaurant. We are all enjoying the many glasses of wine, life stories and shop talk. I am truly enjoying this special evening and my gentleman is as well—he is all smiles. I tell everyone, "Please save room for dessert because this French dinner would not be complete without my The Point of It All Vanilla Crème Brulee and assorted Sorbets." We continue conversing for another 20 minutes or so until everyone has finished their meal. I clear everyone's dinner plates and bring out the platter of desserts. Our guests are enjoying the desserts and more of the wine, while I stack the dirty dishes in the dishwasher and converse with my gentleman in the kitchen for a brief moment. He kisses me gently on my neck and suggests that we should partake in dessert a little later.

My gentleman and I return to the dining room with our guests. The CEO makes a toast to my gentleman and me for our exceptional hospitality, the exquisite cuisine and for making this dinner a night to remember. Everyone concurs and thanks us the same. We tell our guests, that it was our pleasure catering to them this evening.

It's now about 1am and our guests are preparing to leave. My gentleman and I escort them all to the door and thank them for coming. Now that everyone is gone, my gentleman hugs me ever so tightly and thanks me for making him shine tonight. I respond, "you know I love cooking and I will always support you." "Princess, that's why I love you, because you always have my back. The only thing that was missing was seeing you in your sexy apron, but of course you couldn't wear it tonight." "My dear gentleman, I didn't even bring my apron with me tonight." He grabs my hand and walks me to his bedroom then opens one of the doors to his closet and there hanging is one of my sexy aprons. All I can do is smile. "Princess, when you were gathering the groceries earlier today, I grabbed it. Will you oblige me and put it on, so that we can enjoy dessert?" "Yes, my dear gentleman."

I race into the bathroom to freshen up a bit, a few squirts of French perfume and my sexy apron. My gentleman grabs my hand and we head back to the dining room. He has placed the remaining dirty dessert dishes in the dishwasher, turned on some mellow music and wiped down the table. The only thing that remains on the table is the vase containing the

Tempt Your Senses

Vanilla After dinner, devour ice cream flavored with this sweet bean or add a fresh stick to your tea or coffee. It mildly stimulates nerves, making sexual sensations feel even better, once aroused. *Courtesy of www.cosmopolitan.com*

beautiful flower arrangement. "Princess, I want to feed you some dessert because I know that it's your favorite." He begins to feed me, one spoonful at a time and it's so tantalizing. "Come here princess, so I can help you up onto the table. Now lie back and relax." It was such a wonderful view looking up at my handsome gentleman and praying that my head doesn't knock over the flowers. Wow, this table is so strong...

Drink Suggestion(s)

Several bottles of French Champagne and a selection of wines, including: Bordeaux, Burgundy and Condrieu.

Music Suggestion(s)

Make Me Say It Again Girl—The Isley Brothers

If Only For One Night—Luther Vandross

Can't Get Enough of Your Love, Babe—Barry White

Always & Forever—Heatwave

Nothin' Can Change This Love—Sam Cooke

My Boo—Usher & Alicia Keys

All Night Long—SWV

Fantasy #9
FRIENDS & FOOTBALL

This has been a very eventful week both professionally and personally. In addition, my gentleman has asked me to prepare some finger foods for tonight's football game...and of course, I oblige. And, even though, he hasn't said it, he really wants his friends to meet me and to share their thoughts with him. (lol). Secondly, they will also have a chance to enjoy some home cooked food, as well. Because this is football night, the menu doesn't require anything complex, but instead some very simple, yet tasty appetizers. I know that there will be 6 friends in attendance, but I plan on preparing a variety to satisfy everyone's palette. I've come up with—my *Turn Off the Lights Crab Balls*, *It Had to Be You Sweet and Spicy Chicken Wings* and *Spend My Life With You Mini Hamburgers*.

So, I've already purchased the ingredients and will be ready for the 4pm kickoff. So this means that I should be at my gentleman's house by 2pm. Now, what will I wear today, since I will not be able to cook in my apron? I know what —a nice pair of denim jeans, a navy, V-neck cotton t-shirt, a nice beaded, studded belt and my beaded, strappy sandals. So, let's start my normal ritual of a nice hot, soaking bubble bath, then a facial before applying my flawless makeup, a few squirts of French perfume and the application of some scented lotion.

It's 1:30pm. I have loaded the car and I'm headed to my gentleman's home. He hears me pulling into the garage and meets me at the car to grab all the groceries. After he places the bags onto the counter, he gives me a big hug and thanks me again for cooking for the game. He should know by now that I will always support him in any way that I can. Well, I head to the powder room to wash my hands before I start to cook. It's time to get started with today's delectables. My gentleman is going to love today's spread and so will his friends.

Turn Off the Lights Crab Balls

Makes 4 dozen

Prep Time: 15–20 minutes

Cooking Time: 5 minutes

Ingredients:

Vegetable, peanut or canola oil for frying

2 pounds crab meat

2 eggs, whisked

¼ cup mayonnaise

1 1/3 tablespoons mustard

1 medium onion, chopped

2 tablespoons Worcestershire sauce

2 teaspoons Old Bay seasoning

2 cups Everything Flavored Ritz crackers, crushed

Instructions:

1. In a deep, heavy pot, heat oil to 350 degrees F.
2. In a large bowl, combine all the ingredients, ensuring that the crab mixture is mixed well.
3. Form 1-inch balls and place on a large platter.
4. Refrigerate 30 minutes before frying.
5. Deep fry in heated oil for 5-6 minutes, until golden brown.
6. Remove from oil and drain on paper towel lined platter.

It Had To Be You Sweet and Spicy Chicken Wings

(Courtesy of www.shewearsmanyhats.com)

Makes 10 servings

Prep Time: 20 minutes

Cooking Time: 30-40 minutes

Ingredients:

¼ cup plus 2 tablespoons balsamic vinegar

¼ cup plus 2 tablespoons honey

¼ cup plus 2 tablespoons hot chili pepper sauce (or your favorite hot sauce)

6 pounds chicken wings, bone-in

Instructions:

1. Whisk together first three ingredients. Set aside.
2. Preheat grill. Place wings on the grill over low, direct heat. Grill about 15 minutes per side. Then baste chicken with sauce, turn and continue to baste until done and reached desired crispness and color.

Tempt Your Senses

Hot Chilies Capsaicin, a chemical found in fiery peppers, increases circulation to get your blood pumping and stimulates nerve endings, so you'll feel more turned on. *Courtesy of www.cosmopolitan.com*

Spend My Life With You Mini Hamburgers

(Courtesy of www.butterybooks.com)

Makes 4 dozen

Prep Time: 15 minutes

Cooking Time: 12 minutes

Refrigeration Time: 1 hour

Ingredients:

4 pounds ground beef

2 packages onion soup mix

4 eggs, beaten

½ cup dry bread crumbs

½ cup steak sauce

2 teaspoons fajita seasoning

1 teaspoon pepper

48 potato dinner rolls

Condiments: ketchup, mustard, mayonnaise, onions, pickles, lettuce, and cheese

Instructions:

1. Combine all the ingredients, then refrigerate for at least an hour.
2. Preheat oven to 400 degrees F.
3. Grease 2 cookie sheets.
4. Spread the meat mixture evenly on each cookie sheet and press into the pan.

5. Bake for 12 minutes.
6. Cut the meat into 24 squares per pan. Cut the rolls in half and place a burger square in each roll. Top with the desired condiments/garnishes.

About an hour into cooking, three of my gentleman's friends arrive, bearing beer and cognac. He greets them at the door and walks into the kitchen to introduce me. Nice to meet you, Michael, Bob and Jerry—they all want to know what I'm cooking because it smells so good. So, I tell them that I am preparing my Turn Off the Lights Crab Balls, It Had to Be You Sweet and Spicy Chicken Wings and Spend My Life With You Mini Hamburgers. "You're doing all that for us? We feel so privileged." They all congratulate my gentleman and tell him that he's so lucky to have a woman that cooks and looks good doing it. I just smile, as they leave the kitchen and head into the theatre room to have a few drinks before the game.

Since I won't be staying for today's festivities, I will finish preparing everything and then head home. I'm in the home stretch when the doorbell rings. My gentleman quickly makes his way to the door and two additional friends have arrived.

Again he brings them into the kitchen to meet me; "nice to meet you, Lamar and Chris." They respond, "the pleasure is all ours." They are then escorted by my gentleman to the theatre room...and no sooner than he gets to the theater room, the doorbell rings again. It's his last guest, Hamilton...we have our introductions and at last, they have settled into the theatre room. In about 15 minutes, I'll have everything completed, so I can begin preparing the table. Of course, not a meal is eaten without the presence of fresh flowers. I've added the plates, napkins and condiments and in a few, the mouth watering appetizers will make their appearance.

Now everything is ready! I head down to the theatre room to speak with my gentleman for a bit before leaving. We walk back to the eat-in kitchen and he samples one of the crab balls. "Princess, these are so good that I think I'll have another." He hugs me again and thanks me for taking the time to cater to his friends today. I love him and I love cooking so it's never a problem for me. I jump into my car and head home. After getting home, I undress, put on some mellow music and relax with a nice glass of Moscato.

Before I know it, I've fallen asleep. Several hours have passed and my phone rings—it's my dear gentleman. "Princess, are you sleeping?" I respond, "Yes, I came home, undressed and had a glass or two of Moscato and before I knew it, I'd fallen asleep."

"I just wanted to thank you again for cooking today and to let you know that my friends all think that you are classy, sassy and sexy. They told me that I should never let you go. I love you princess, please get some sleep." "Good night, my dear gentleman; I love you, too!"

Drink Suggestion(s)

Several bottles of domestic and imported beer

Brandy

Cognac

Fantasy #10
THE PROPOSAL

It's about 9am Saturday morning and today my gentleman and I are heading out on his yacht to enjoy the beautiful weather. We are excited about taking the yacht out for the first time this Summer. But, let me stop to tell you about my gentleman's luxury on water, named "The Gentleman." It has a fully-equipped kitchen with stainless steel appliances and will accommodate up to 20 guests as there are 10 suites. There is even a VIP cabin for special guests and the four upper decks are connected by an elevator with views of the ocean. And, last but not least, the Master Suite has two marble bathrooms, a Jacuzzi, theatre room with a 72-inch television, wet bar and a terrace. It's nice to know that even though we both work very hard, when we play, we know how to play hard, too!

We decided yesterday that he'd pick me up at 11am and we

would head to the dock. One big change is that he said I didn't have to worry about preparing a meal this time. He had it all under control. I turn my attention to the other thing that brings him joy—me! I definitely want to look pretty for my gentleman. I've finally jumped out the bed and decided to take a nice bubble bath. I soak for about 25 minutes; dry off and apply lotion, then complete my beauty rituals because I always aim to please. I spray a few mists of French perfume, apply my flawless natural looking makeup and lastly, carefully add a very pretty, pink lip gloss. Now what will I wear today? I know the perfect dress—a sexy, pink strappy mini sundress that accentuates my body perfectly and my silver, gladiator sandals. It's 10:45am and I'm ready! Oops, let me not forget my sexy apron! I folded it and placed it in my purse. My gentleman is calling now. "Princess, I'll be there in 10 minutes." I'm excited. "Sounds great!"

He's here, so I head downstairs; lock the house and jump into his convertible. Our wonderful Saturday has begun and we are all smiles. "So, my dear gentleman what's for lunch?" "Well Princess, I've had my staff to stock the fridge and bar, so we'll eat as soon as we are on board. We are about 10 minutes away from the dock." I always look forward to sailing on "The Gentleman" because it really makes me feel like a princess!

We walk on board. "Good Morning, Captain!" When my gentleman is on board, he is in charge and his captain takes care of the navigating. This allows us to enjoy quality time and all of the yacht amenities. I run up to the Master Suite to place my bag down. I always forget how luxurious the Suite really is . . . I really think I could actually stay here on a permanent basis (lol). I admire the view from the Suite window and then remember how hungry I am. I head down to the first floor to the kitchen/dining area to talk to my gentleman about lunch. However, the closer I get, the more I smell an amazing food aroma. "Princess, come here for a minute!"

"My dear gentleman, what's going on?" "Princess, you are always cooking for me, so I wanted to surprise you today. So, I hired a caterer to prepare lunch for us. We are having stuffed shrimp, beef wellington, baked chicken, au gratin potatoes, string beans, corn bread and for dessert—peach cobbler." I'm speechless. "You had them prepare all this food for just the two of us?" "Well, not exactly!" I'm puzzled. "Well, what do you mean?" All of a sudden about 30 family members and friends come out of their suites with smiles on their faces. Again I ask, "My dear gentleman, what's going on?"

"Princess, not only do I want to cater to you today, but I'd like to cater to you for the rest of our lives. My heart can't beat without you. He pulls out a 6-carat, canary yellow diamond engagement ring from his pocket and gets down on one knee. . . Princess, will you marry me? I can't believe what is happening. I begin to cry as I look around the room at the faces of my family and friends.

Then I look back into my wonderful man's eyes and begin to shout, "Yes, my dear Gentleman! Yes!"

Music Suggestion(s)

Love Never Felt So Good — Michael Jackson
Love Makes Things Happen — Babyface & Pebbles
Love Saw It — Karen White
I Will Always Love You — Whitney Houston
The One — Tamar Braxton
I Do Love You — GQ
At Last — Etta James

ABOUT THE
AUTHOR

Myra C. Harris

Myra loves romance and courtship. She believes in the pursuit of happiness by spending time with a special someone and family, while enjoying one of her great passions—cooking. She is a talented and creative woman who has been successful in many different endeavors.

She began her career working as a dedicated professional at the Central Intelligence Agency (CIA). She then went on to become a compliance associate in the legal department of a Fortune 500 company, and ultimately mastering skills as a seasoned, technical trainer. Myra used these skills to become a successful and sought after trainer for several top rated law firms and other government agencies. Not only do her writing skills extend to this book of recipes and fantasies, but she has also written hundreds of training and compliance manuals.

Myra has a son and lives in Alexandria, Virginia.

Visit www.letaypublishing.com
for information about this and other titles.

CPSIA information can be obtained at www.ICGtesting.com
Printed in the USA
BVOW11*0004060515

399130BV00002B/2/P